D1444346

Braving -the- Storm

Written by Jenny McCray
Illustrated by Jessica Donehue

Book Design & Production: Columbus Publishing Lab • www.ColumbusPublishingLab.com

Paperback ISBN 978-1-63337-173-6 • E-book ISBN 978-1-63337-174-3

Printed in the United States of America
1 3 5 7 9 10 8 6 4 2

For Lindsay—who braved the storm with purpose, faith and grace.
You will forever be my real life superhero who never needed a cape.

We all have that one, true friend
Who rises above the rest.
That mate who won't leave your side,
Even when put to the test.

My special pal is Pierre.
He is simply one of a kind.
Covered in quills from head to toe—
Pierre the porcupine!

For as long as I can remember,
He's been my trusty friend.
Beside me through every adventure.
Beside me at each day's end.

He puts me in fits of laughter
When he does his porcupine wiggle.
He arches his back, fluffs out his spikes
And makes his whole body j^{i}g$_g$l$_e$!

But his wiggle is more than amusement—
It's useful when fighting wars,
And Pierre always travels with me
To brave the great outdoors.

We're make believe superheroes,
Defying all odds and reason.
A fearless crime fighting duo,
Braving evils of every season.

Our daydreams keep us busy
With every season's turn,
And adventures call upon us
To assist with climate concern.

My mighty superhero cape

Gives **STRENGTH** on any mission,

While Pierre and
his spike-a-roos

Help
crush
the competition.

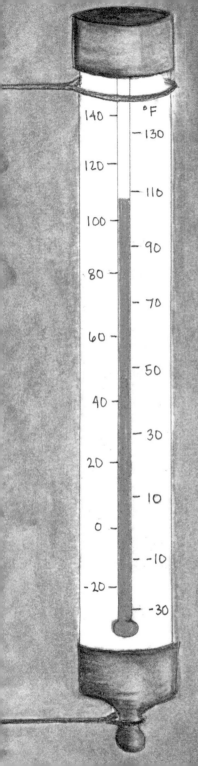

Snow days are never routine.
Rainy days never boring.
Imagination fuels us,
And sends our minds exploring.

The days are getting longer.
The heat is on the rise.
Mornings are kissed with summer dew—
Nights glow with fireflies.

It hasn't rained for many weeks.
There's not a cloud in the sky.
Blaze McFury is in pursuit
And he wants to see us fry!

McFury is red with anger.
He's cooking up quite a plan.
A ball of fire-filled fury—
Blazing anything he can.

It's time to tame his temper.
McFury has crossed the line.
Pierre and I get moving,
For it's OUR TURN to shine!

We jump on our hero-mobile
And speed to the corner store,
Then buy up the water balloons
And jet back out the door.

We hightail it
   home to safety,
Careful to dodge
   the sun's rays.

We quickly get
   down to business!

There's no time for delays!

11

We head to the water faucet
To fill the balloons with care.
Huddling close together,
We each do our fair share.

We gather our swollen bundle,
And hoard them onto my cape.
We wrap them snug and tight,
Ensuring that none escape.

Venturing through the yard
We spot the tallest tree,
And test each branch's strength,
As we climb them carefully.

14

As McFury throws his heat,
We're protected in the shade.
Our attack is about to begin!
These heroes aren't afraid!

We perch in a sturdy spot
Staking claim to our space.
Pierre shimmies *slowly*,
Then rapidly picks up the pace.

Waltzing to the branch's edge
He hip hops to and fro,
Plumping his prickly pokers
He signals me to throw.

Swinging my cape like a lasso
In figure eights through the air,
I wind up the sack of soakers
And hurl them toward Pierre.

His daggers burst the balloons.
Water cascades like the rain.
It splashes over McFury
Halting his fiery campaign.

The sweltering summer's been saved!
We feel the sizzle subside.
Our partnership packs a punch!
NOTHING can stop our stride!

New seasons spark new adventures
For me and my faithful friend.
We're always on high alert
To protect and to defend.

The birds are migrating south
In patterns across the skies.
Summer is winding down.
We're in for another surprise.

As autumn paints the trees
In colors fiery bright,
The air turns cool and damp—
A hurricane's taking flight!

The sky transforms to gray.
The clouds are rolling in.
The trees begin to whisper
And windmills start to spin.

His name is Hurricane Higgins.
He's out to cause a scene.
He's hatched an evil plot
To ruin Halloween!

Pierre and I have a plan.
Higgins stands no chance!
We're armed with my trusty cape
And the feared "porcupine dance"!

We can't let Higgins prevail
With his rainy winds of force.
It's time to challenge this monster!
We WON'T be blown off course!

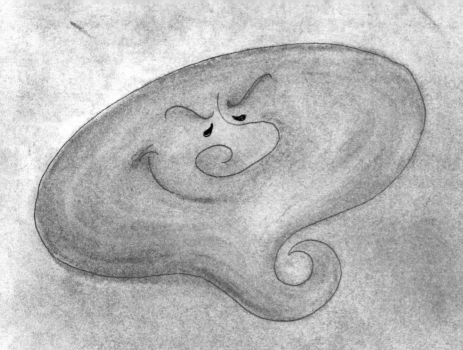

We bolt to the neighborhood playground.
There's not a person in sight.
We quietly wait in the tube slide
For Higgins' monsoon to ignite.

He's gusting something fierce.
The air is sopping wet.
It's time for us to save the day
And stop this wicked threat!

My cape drapes over
our faces,
Shielding us from
the hard rain.

Pierre climbs
up the slide,
Gripping the
polished terrain.

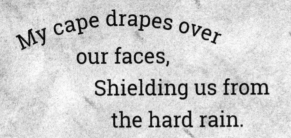

He bounces onto the bars
Trying to steady his stance.
He gingerly catches his footing,
Then shakes and breaks into his dance.

Pierre whirls round in circles—
He's consistent in his routine.
Higgins moves in like a freight train
With the force of a mighty machine!

24

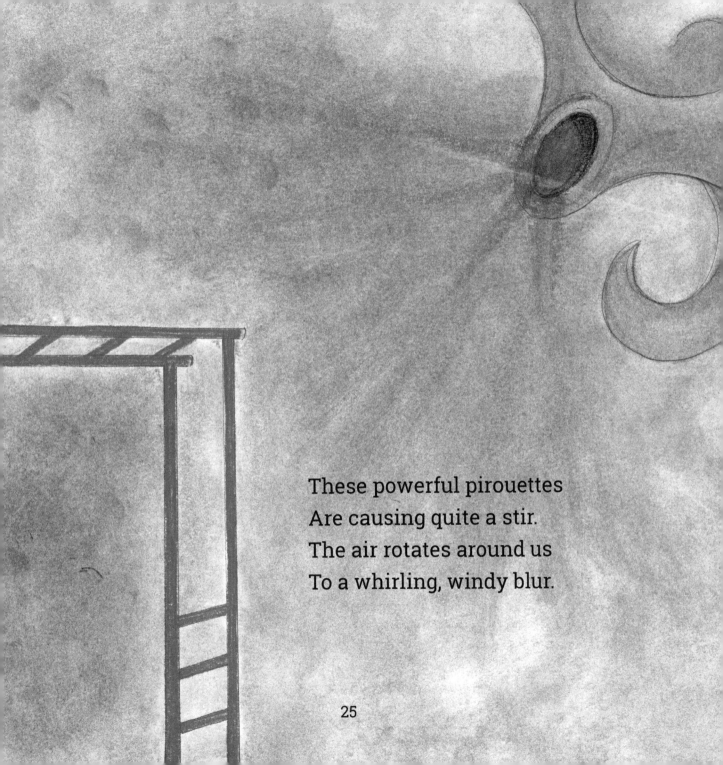

These powerful pirouettes
Are causing quite a stir.
The air rotates around us
To a whirling, windy blur.

Pierre twirls onto the ground
Ready for resistance.
I knot my cape to the swing set
Spotting Higgins in the distance.

Higgins attempts to floor us,
But Pierre just spins and spins.
His quills sway every which way
Like a thousand spiraling pins.

26

Higgins blows back with a vengeance,
But his attempt falls short of his aim.
Pierre spins Higgins out of town
Quicker than when he came!

Another triumphant mission.
We're quite the unstoppable team!
We've conquered another threat,
And squashed another scheme.

A new season to play pretend
Brings new perils for me and Pierre.

Winter weather's approaching—
We can see our breath in the air.

Today a polar wind's blowing.
The ground is blanketed white.
Old Man Winter is at the door
And he's looking to pick a fight.

Pierre and I get bundled,

Preparing to face what's ahead,

Then quietly crawl through the kitchen

To sneak out the back door, instead.

Together we dash toward a tree,
Trampling through the dense snow.
My cape drums against my back
With every blustery blow.

We swiftly spring into action
Molding ammo to perfection.
We pack the snowballs tightly
Proud of our chilled protection.

I gather the snowballs with care—
Two by two from the stack.
Pierre readily bares his barbs
And I stick them onto his back.

With the final snowballs in place
We're armed with our defense.
We're ready to march into battle!
Our ambush can finally commence!

Slouching low to the ground
We tiptoe toward the front yard.
Then rushing at Old Man Winter
We catch the grouch off guard!

The cold wind swirls around us
As Pierre shifts in his stance.
Moving and grooving his body
He does his porcupine dance.

The ice man aims to chill us
But his efforts are too late.
As the snowballs launch from Pierre
Winter is met with his fate.

We breathe a sigh of relief.
We've both come out unscathed.
Another adventure behind us
And another season saved!

But one day something happened—
An attack we did not expect.
Pierre was matched with a villain
Neither of us could deflect.

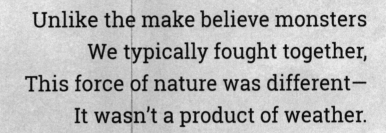

Unlike the make believe monsters
We typically fought together,
This force of nature was different—
It wasn't a product of weather.

This thief was a unique breed,
The kind that strikes for no reason.
It chooses its targets at random
And invades during any season.

It's a germ so meek and quiet,
It moves in calm and quick.
A rebel whose only cause
Is to make its victims feel sick.

Pierre wondered, "Why me?"
But this scummy bug gave no answer.
And it couldn't be fought with the wiggles
Of my friend, the porcupine dancer.

36

So Pierre took a magic serum
To help him wage his attack.
But this elixir came with a price—
It took the quills from off his back.

Pierre felt so defeated,
Though he sent this sickness packing,
Because now that his pokers were gone
He felt that his powers were lacking.

So he came to me one day
Wearing a frown of despair,
And announced our twosome was over
Now that his back was bare.

He thought he wouldn't be helpful
Through our superhero thrills,
Because a porcupine couldn't beat bad guys
Doing a wiggle without any quills.

He told me he was sorry,
Then hung his weary head.
So I put my arm around him,
And this is what I said:

38

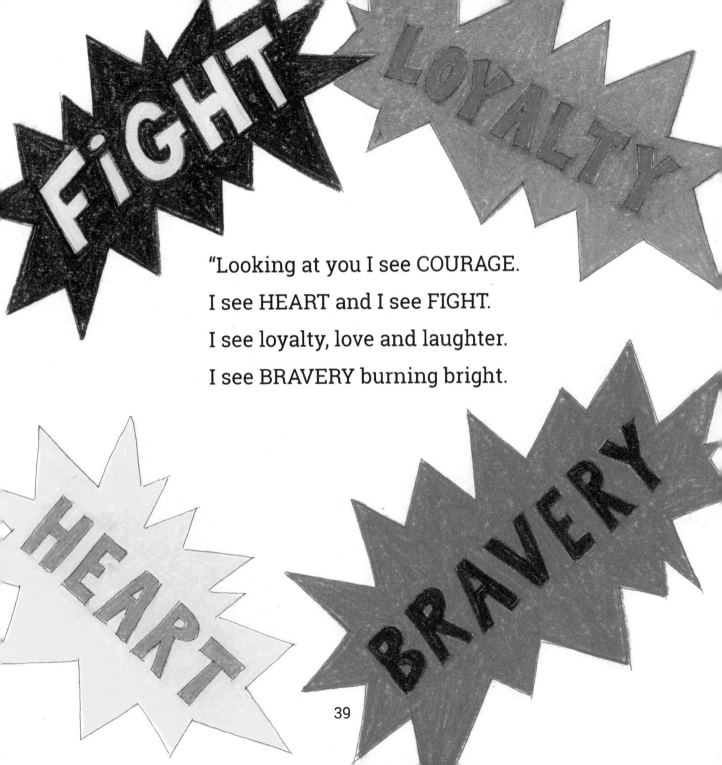

"Looking at you I see COURAGE.

I see HEART and I see FIGHT.

I see loyalty, love and laughter.

I see BRAVERY burning bright.

39

"Our alliance endured the seasons
So together we'll weather this storm.
And if the forecast looks too frigid
I'll be there to keep you warm.

"Wear my cape upon your back
When your journey feels too long.
It will give you the superpowers
To feel confident, bold and strong.

"Your spines don't make you special—
You're special for who you are.
Your outside doesn't define you,
Your INSIDE makes you a star!

"You are a hero where it matters most
In that place where courage seeps.
You are a hero because of your heart
And our brotherhood is for keeps.

"No matter what we're faced with
We'll conquer it together.
Because heroes never falter,
And friendships fare all weather."

So when a storm cloud lingers
And you feel it hovering low,
Hold tight to those who love you
And NEVER let them go!

Remember, life is full of storms
That leave us soaked with fear,
But seasons of change are waiting
And rainbows will soon appear.

CPSIA information can be obtained
at www.ICGtesting.com
Printed in the USA
BVOW07s0753101117
500044BV00028B/229/P